WRITTEN AND ILLUSTRATED BY
CARYN MOTTILLA

Dale and the Valentine Star

Dale and the Valentine Star
The Patio Club™
Published by Open Window Publishing
Castle Rock, CO

Publisher's Cataloging-in-Publication data

Names: Mottilla, Caryn, author.
Title: Dale and the Valentine star / by Caryn Mottilla.
Description: First trade paperback original edition. Also available as an ebook. | Castle Rock [Colorado] : Open Window Publishing, 2019. | Series: The Patio Club.
Identifiers: ISBN 978-0-9997471-3-1
Subjects: LCSH: Old age—Fiction. | Valentine's Day—Fiction. | Short stories.
BISAC: FICTION / General.
Classification: LCC PS374.O43 | DDC 813–dc22

Cover design by Caryn Mottilla

QUANTITY PURCHASES: Schools, companies, professional groups, clubs, and other organizations may qualify for special terms when ordering quantities of this title. For information, email ThePatioClub@gmail.com.

OPEN WINDOW
PUBLISHING

The Patio Club® is dedicated to the men and women in assisted living communities, memory and Hospice care who have listened to the adventures of The Patio Club®. They expressed their hope for these stories to be published and shared with others across the country.

An Introduction to The Patio Club

The Patio Club was originally formed by two sets of sisters—Elaine and Adele from New Jersey, and Betty and Mildred from Kentucky. The women were young when they met in the 1940s. The years passed by, and later in life, the four adventurous women made a pact that after they died they would meet up and visit retirement and assisted living communities. After they passed away, they came to Happy Visions Retirement Home and liked it so much they decided to stay.

The women call themselves "The Patio Club," because they sit outside on the patio of Happy Visions. Each day, Elaine, Adele,

Betty and Mildred are surrounded by colorful sparkles, and they meet a steady stream of interesting visitors and residents who pass through Happy Visions on their way to unknown destinations.

One amazing thing is that the Patio Club can look to the sky and watch a video of each person's life. This precious gift lets the Patio Club understand the unique story that each person carries with them.

Dale and the Valentine Star

IT WAS THE MIDDLE OF FEBRUARY BUT YOU would not know this by looking around the grounds outside of Happy Visions Retirement Home. Warm weather colored the buds on trees and crab grass boasted of being the first of the grasses to turn green.

Outside of Happy Visions, the four delightful women of the Patio Club sat in the unseasonably warm February breeze. Elaine, Adele, Betty and Mildred listened as birds cheerfully called to each other. It surely looked like spring was on the way, but the women knew better than to fall for Mother Nature's practical joke that winter was over.

Inside of Happy Visions, the subject of Valentine's Day peppered the conversations taking place in the dining room as residents socialized during meals. In the craft room, the staff prepared art supplies for residents to make valentines to exchange with each other.

As the women of the Patio Club sat outside in the first light of day, they noticed a young man dressed in blue jeans and a red and white checked shirt. He was hanging a valentine wreath from the back door. "Good morning, ladies! My name is Dale. I've come to visit someone very special who lives here. Happy Valentine's Day." Before the women could even ask a question, Dale was gone.

"What a nice young man," said Adele. "How kind of him to hang a valentine wreath."

Betty suddenly said, "Good Lord!" What's with these wreaths? I swear there is a now a wreath for *every* holiday and month!

Elaine, Adele, Betty and Mildred enjoyed new mysteries and the people who came with them. The four women

quickly left the chairs where they were sitting and walked over to the wreath that the young man had just hung.

As the women looked more closely at the wreath, they could tell it was very old. Pink and red ribbons were woven together to form the wreath's shape. Glittering red hearts and cardboard pieces of candy brought the wreath to life. Mildred laughed and said, "There is no telling how many people over the years have tried to eat that cardboard candy!"

In the center of the wreath was a sparkling gold star. Although the wreath seemed very old, the star still sparkled. In fact, the Patio Club noticed that the star seemed to sparkle even *more* brightly as the light of dawn danced over the patio.

Adele remarked that a gold star at the center of a valentine wreath was strange. "Who would put a star on a valentine wreath?" she asked the others.

Elaine looked at the wreath and it made her think back to Valentine's Day when she was a child. She said,

"I remember when we were kids, we had very little, but we still found a way to find small valentine treasures, like the star. It's funny. It seems that when we had so little, small surprises brought great delight."

Mildred said, "We had to be very creative for Valentine's Day. One year, we put rhubarb stocks in warm water to color our valentines. The water turned red and we dipped our valentines in it. What a mess we made!"

Betty laughed as she listened to her sister Mildred. "I recall you always hid your homemade valentines for me so I had to go on a treasure hunt to find them. That was fun!"

Adele told the others that Elaine had a knack for finding pennies—even during the Great Depression. She said, "Elaine would wrap one penny in red paper and give it to me." She smiled and added, "And back in those days, *one penny* bought a lot of candy!"

As the women reminisced about their early valentines, a spark suddenly flew from the gold star in the middle of the faded valentine wreath. The women gasped with surprise!

Distracted by the spark, none of the women noticed the young man named Dale as he stood watching them from the far side of the patio. A shadow of shimmering pink and red sparkles surrounded him. Dale laughed with amusement as the women of the Patio Club *jumped* when they saw the spark fly from the valentine star.

The women of the Patio Club did not know it yet, but Dale had come to Happy Visions Retirement Home to give a special valentine message to Eleanor. She was in the Memory Unit.

Each day, Eleanor sat in a wooden rocking chair with a colorful quilt in her lap as she looked out the window in her room. Eleanor found simple pleasure in watching how life parades in front of those who take the time to observe it.

Although Eleanor forgot she had made the quilt, that kept her warm each day, she never forgot Valentine's Day. It was one of her favorite holidays.

Eleanor could see Dale each time he came to visit her at Happy Visions. Even though Dale had died a few years back, he told Eleanor that he would visit her often and signal her with the gold, sparkling valentine star.

Several people would often see Eleanor laughing as she looked out of the window. They could not understand what Eleanor found so funny! Whenever Dale came to visit, he would make Eleanor laugh when he put the gold, sparkling valentine star on squirrels, on trees or on the maintenance crew when they shoveled sidewalks or mowed the lawn.

The women of the Patio Club stood staring at the gold star in the center of the worn valentine wreath. They had never before looked to the video in the sky to see the story of an *object*.

Mildred suddenly said, "This sparking valentine star and wreath must tell some kind of story". "Let's see if we can discover what it is."

As the women of the Patio Club turned to look to the sky, they suddenly saw Dale smiling at them as he stood on the other side of the patio. His happy smile sent a streak of pink sparkles skidding across the patio toward the four startled women.

Just then, the women of the Patio Club looked up and saw Eleanor through the window to her room. She was laughing and seemed quite amused.

It might surprise people to know that Eleanor was capable of observing something this entertaining! Even if Eleanor were to tell someone, they probably would *not* believe her. That is what made it so special. The only one who knew Eleanor's secret was Dale, and now the women of the Patio Club knew it too. But who was Dale?

Elaine, Adele, Mildred and Betty quickly looked up to the sky as the colorful video came to life. They saw two young children playing. The boy looked to be about eight years old and the girl was closer to seven. The children were out in the countryside, and the only thing in sight

was an old, white farmhouse that stood behind them. It was surrounded by a wooden fence and acres of land.

Hanging from the door of the white farmhouse was a homemade wreath. It was the same valentine wreath that Dale had hung earlier from the patio door. The young girl in the video said, "Dale, Mom just put up the valentine wreath she made. Don't eat the cardboard candy on it. (*Dale had tried to eat the cardboard candy the year before.*) I think Mom's wreath will last until we are old. Do you?"

The young boy named Dale laughed and said, "Maybe, Eleanor." He had a mischievous smile on his face and looked like he was up to something! Dale's favorite holiday was Valentine's Day, and he loved surprising people that day. As the women watched, they saw Dale reach into his red and white checked shirt pocket, pull out a valentine card and hand it to his sister Eleanor.

In the center of the valentine card was a firecracker from the Fourth of July. The women of the Patio Club

clearly heard Dale say to his sister Eleanor, "*Don't* tell mom about the sparkler or we will both get into trouble!"

The four women of the Patio Club laughed at Dale's comment. Elaine exclaimed, "It must be the same Dale that hung the valentine wreath here. The old farmhouse must have been where Dale and Eleanor lived when they were growing up."

The video continued and showed Dale when he was a young teenager—about fourteen years old. Dale was on a ladder at the back of their white farmhouse, and he had just begun to paint it *red*! He thought it would be a nice surprise for his mom for Valentine's Day that year. Needless to say, this surprise did not go over too well with his mother! She made him stop after he painted a few red streaks on the house, and he had to use a towel to clean the mess.

Next, the video showed Dale serving in the military. That year for Valentine's Day, Dale surprised Eleanor by sending her the valentine wreath their mother had

made. He put a battery-operated star in the middle of the valentine wreath. Dale told his sister it seemed safer than a firecracker.

The video closed with Dale's funeral. Eleanor put the valentine wreath on Dale's grave that day. Soon after, she watched with amusement as she saw a pink heart-shaped cloud around the sun. Eleanor knew that even on the day of his funeral, Dale was still surprising her.

Elaine, Adele, Betty and Mildred were so happy! They looked around, and Dale was nowhere in sight. When they looked to the window in Eleanor's room, they saw bright red sparkles in the shape of a heart surrounding the glass window.

Later that day for dinner, the cooks made pink mashed potatoes and red pudding for dessert. Some of the residents *refused* to eat anything pink or red! After dinner, the residents exchanged the valentine cards they had made for each other earlier that day. Even Eleanor had made one. She told her caregivers that she needed to have one just in case her brother Dale stopped by to visit her.

Later that evening, Elaine, Adele, Betty and Mildred went outside as the last light of day disappeared from the sky. They looked to Eleanor's room and through the window, they saw Dale handing Eleanor a valentine card. Eleanor read it and smiled with delight. Then Eleanor handed Dale the valentine card she had made for him earlier that day. Dale kissed Eleanor on the top of her head and he was gone.

The following morning, the staff caring for Eleanor noticed that her homemade valentine card for her brother Dale was gone. In Eleanor's window, hanging from a red ribbon was a valentine card from Dale. The staff had no idea how the card from Eleanor's brother had gotten there. On the front of the card was a pink heart that would occasionally light up. The card made everyone who saw it smile.

After sunrise, the women of the Patio Club noticed that the old valentine wreath with the gold sparkling star was now gone from the patio door. As the curious women looked to the sky, the video began to play and showed

Dale standing on a ladder that was leaning against the old farmhouse. He was holding a paintbrush and red paint dripped from it. Dale was almost finished *painting* the farmhouse *red* just like he tried to do many years before for his mother for Valentine's Day. Dale was waving joyfully to the women of the Patio Club as they watched him.

On the front door of the *now* red farmhouse was the old valentine wreath with the sparkling gold star at the center of it. The cardboard candy was still on the wreath. Eleanor had been right. The wreath had lasted until they were old *and so had the cardboard candy!*

As the video closed against the cloudy February sky, it suddenly changed into a homemade valentine card from Dale to the four women of the Patio Club. A bright pink shooting star flew from the card and streaked high over their heads across the late winter sky. Dale was still enjoying surprising special people for Valentine's Day!

Happy valentine surprises from the Patio Club!

The End.

The Patio Club's Story

IN NOVEMBER OF 2016, I began writing fictional stories for retirement and assisted living communities. This occurred because of a simple request from an older gentleman in his 80s who asked if I could write a story about people "their age." Writing and telling stories has always come easily to me. I happily said , "yes." I was excited at the challenge and have written a story each month since then. They are about a fictional retirement/ assisted living community named *Happy Visions*. Each month I read to retirement and assisted living communities. The joy of doing this is overwhelming.

In July of 2017, I was reading to a group of older women as they sat outside *on the patio* in the shade. The women's ages reached up to 95. When I left the patio that day, I decided at that moment to write a story for them called "The Patio Club." The series began with that story.

The stories I write come effortlessly to me. It is as if I am divinely inspired. As I began writing the first story in the Patio Club series, I was so surprised as I watched the story come to life. It is the story of two sets of sisters, Elaine and Adele from New Jersey, and Mildred and Betty from Kentucky. They made a pact that when they died they would meet up and visit retirement and assisted living communities.

Imagine my surprise—because in real life Elaine and Adele (sisters) were my aunts from New Jersey, and Betty (my mother) and Mildred (my aunt) were sisters from Kentucky! My Aunt Mildred was the last one to join The Patio Club. She passed away earlier in 2017. The Patio Club™ stories now touch people from around the country and hopefully someday from around the world.

My dream is that The Patio Club™ series will be read to the people in assisted living, memory and Hospice care communities. As I read each month to these special people, I realized that it is often difficult to visit loved ones who are in the assisted living population. What I have found is that reading a story seems to transform everyone from the reader to the listener. I have seen people with all kinds of health challenges perk up when listening to the joyful adventures of The Patio Club™. They are in the present moment as they listen and during that time there is nothing wrong with them.

My wish is that people will take the adventure of reading a story (about 12 to 15 minutes) from The Patio Club Series to a loved one. It will transform the visit from one where it may be difficult to find something to talk about, to one where both the reader and listener are moved beyond words.

With gratitude and love,

- Caryn

Acknowledgments

THE PATIO CLUB is dedicated to my aunts Elaine, Adele, Mildred, and my mother Betty. Although the characters in the Patio Club are fictional, they are based on these important women who impacted my life.

Special thanks to my sons Carson and Cooper, as well as, family and friends who have listened to these stories. They have enthusiastically cheered for me to follow my dream to write and illustrate stories that bring joy and adventure to the lives of others.

Finally, I am grateful to God for the gifts He has given me to serve the people in assisted living, memory and Hospice care.

About the Author

CARYN BEGAN WRITING children's stories for her children in the 1990s. In 2016, as she read children's stories to assisted living communities, residents asked her to write a story "for people their age." That was how the adventure of writing for the adult and assisted population began.

Since that time, Caryn has written a monthly series called The Patio Club®. It takes place at a retirement home/assisted living community named Happy

Visions. The Patio Club™ are the first stories published by Caryn for that age group. The stories have captured the attention of people of all ages across the country.

The Patio Club™ stories are a bridge between the reader and the listener. Family and friends that visit assisted living, memory and Hospice care communities may struggle for something to talk about. Reading a story like The Patio Club™ to these special residents takes them on an adventure without them ever having to leave the room. It creates an opening for some interesting conversations!

Caryn lives in Colorado. She has two grown sons, Carson and Cooper

www.ingramcontent.com/pod-product-compliance
Lightning Source LLC
Chambersburg PA
CBHW041609120626

46551CB00002B/364